"Secrets, Pain, Murder and Revenge"

PRODUCT
OF MY MOTHER'S
Pain

TAMARA S. LAGUINS

PRODUCT of My MOTHER'S Pain

BOOK 1 (SERIES)

Tamara S. La Guins

Pure Thoughts Publishing, LLC

www.purethoughtspublishing.com

ISBN13:978-1-943409-73-0

Printed in the United States of America

Table of Contents

Dedication

First and foremost, this book is dedicated to my Lord and Savior, the Holy Spirit that lives within and guides me in everything, the One who gave me the vision and told me to write, the Giver and Sustainer of my Life, the Lover of my Soul, thank You with my whole-heart.

Secondly, to my eldest daughter, Delaina, you came in my room one night after hearing me pour out and the story was manifested. You read, and I saw the sparkle in your eyes. It was that spark that ignited the fire the Holy Ghost had placed in me to use the circumstances as my paper and the pain as my ink. I love you more than you could possibly understand.

To my other babies, Taeghen, Delrius, and my God-daughter Jayda, you made me smile when I wanted to cry, pray when I just wanted to hellishly fight, and laugh until I ached; Mommy needed it all. I love you all beyond measure.

To My Mommy: Your journey and the pain you endured were not in vain. You are the epitome of strength, and I appreciated the lessons I learned from you allowing me to watch you play the hand life dealt you. YOU ARE A WINNER, and you are my hero. "You excel them all" (Proverbs 31:29).

Finally, to my husband: It has never been easy for us individually, and we have had battles to fight together, sometimes fighting each other, but together we have overcome enemies, pushed past the pain of losing "frienemies," and risen together. We have and we will continue to do all things unto the Lord together. Thank you for your P.U.S.H.ing and encouragement. I love you "Forever", and there is nothing anyone can do about it.

That's my story, and I am sticking to it. For I have been created by God to love the Hell out of you (sound familiar? LOL).

Prologue

My mama was a child of God. Lord knows she wasn't a saint as saints go today, but she was a child of God. Tilda Larain Mitchell was her name. She wasn't high yellow like some of them, but she was a beautiful woman with smooth -mocha chocolate skin. She always had her hair styled, thanks to one of her own many talents, and clothes just seemed to fit to her like a hand to a real leather glove. She made the heads of single men spin, the eyes of married men wonder, and the women loved to hate her. Not only was Mama beautiful, she was intelligent and capable of speaking her mind so that there was no one who could claim they did not understand. My mother was the type of woman some women wanted to be like and others envied.

Children were afraid of her but drawn to her and loved her even more. Men? Men hated her but lusted after her. Many would say the need to be loved for who she was by those she loved the most was the thorn in my mama's flesh. They were only half right. Over time, the thorn in my mama's flesh would slowly and painfully reveal itself.

Now, Mama was also a bold woman. This didn't sit too well with most folks, men and women alike. She never cared too much for titles and didn't mind telling even the holiest of people that they were wrong and the truth wasn't in them. (I'm not exaggerating either because I witnessed it on more than one occasion.) She wasn't afraid to let people know what was on her mind and would always be the first to admit when she was wrong.

Everybody in the small town of Midtown, Arkansas thought she was as mean as a rattlesnake, except for the few folks that took the time to get to know her. Mama wasn't as mean as she let on. I learned later in life that this was just what the fancy psychologist called a defense mechanism.

Actually, my mama was very sensitive and carried around a lot of unspoken pain. I know because I used to sit outside her bedroom door at night and listen to her cry and talk to God until she fell asleep. Sometimes she cried so hard, I thought that she was going to shake the walls of our little shotgun house down.

Every now and then, when she forgot to lock it, I would push her bedroom door open just a little bit so that I could make out her silhouette. I had no fear of her seeing me because she would be sitting on her knees in the middle of her bedroom in total darkness. Only the light from her stereo would be shining, but it was just enough to help me see where she was and what she was doing. I didn't worry about her hearing me either because even though she wasn't crying very loudly, her pain was so intense that I don't believe she could hear anything but the breaking of her own heart.

She never called God by one of those names that I heard the preachers and all the saints say: Jehovah, Yahweh, Father, Alpha and Omega. No, I believe Mama saw God in a way none of them or even I did. Mama just called out to "DADDY". Sometimes that's all she would say. She would rock on her knees back and forth; back and forth; back and forth for hours in the night and only cry, "DADDY".

I was young, perhaps about eleven or twelve, when I sat outside Mama's bedroom door one night. I am not sure what made me go to her bedroom door the first time I did it, but once I found out what she was doing, it seemed like I had to be there every night. See, I knew what other people didn't know about my mama: she had a hole in her heart. She had an emptiness that no one on this side of Heaven could fill. I'm not sure if she was born with it or if it was caused by the people on this side of Heaven, but it was there.

Sometimes, I begged her to go to church with Me-Ma and Pa-pa, but she would just smile and say, "My sweet baby, church don't won't everybody, but they sho' need you." Then, she would send me on with my grandparents. I overheard someone say that she refused to step foot in another church after the incident, but she never stopped reading her Bible, praying, and even telling people about God when she took the notion to (mostly after she had consumed what she called "liquid courage").

See, I knew something else people didn't know about my mama: she was one of God's anointed. I didn't realize it until I heard the preacher talking about a prophet named Elijah and a young man named Elisha. The preacher said that Elijah knew that God was getting ready to take him to Heaven, so he told the young Elisha to ask him for what he wanted. Elisha saw the power, the anointing, of the prophet and asked for a double portion of that same power. Elijah warned him that what he had asked for was hard, but if that is what he truly wanted, then if he was there when Elijah was taken by God, he could have what he wanted. I immediately thought about my mama and me. She may not have called herself a prophet, but she had power. Power, I think, she didn't even realize she had, and maybe that's why that hole in her heart was never filled. Mama's own well of tears could never even fill that hole in her heart, and afraid as I was, I knew I was her Elisha.

She never knew I was there, but I had to be at her door. Perhaps it was because I was afraid that on one of those nights, God would relieve my mama of her pain once and for all. And perhaps, I wanted a double portion of the power that I knew my mama had. At least I thought I did. I made it my duty to be by her bedroom door every night because I knew she was going to heaven one day. Regardless of what folks said about her, or how they treated her; she was going to be with her "DADDY".

I just knew that one of those nights, her DADDY was going to take her into His arms and never let her go. I was certain that on one of those nights, my mama was going to believe that she was, yet again, alone with God; she would believe that she had died alone, but I was not going to let that happen. My mama felt alone in this world, probably all of her life but I was not going to allow her to die that way. I knew that I was going to be right there. I didn't realize that it would be some time later, but that's exactly how it would be: I would be right there when my mama's most heartfelt prayer was answered.

<u>Chapter 1</u>

When God Speaks to a Child, Someone Ought to Take Notice

"Before I formed you in the womb I knew you, before you were born I set you apart; I appointed you as a prophet to the nations."
Jeremiah 1:5

*T*ilda Larain made her presence known even in the womb. Her mama had more gas than the local convenient store sold, and she had more heartburn than the grocery store had Tums to relieve. It was a most uncomfortable pregnancy if you let my Me-ma tell it. There was only one thing that calmed my unborn mama as she grew in my grandmother's womb: the sweet sound of her mother's singing. Me-ma says she couldn't just sing anything to Tilda like she could her four other girls. Her second oldest child only wanted to hear hymns, and her favorite seemed to be "Guide Me Over, Thy Great Jehovah." Me-ma said she could practically feel my mama get comfortable and fall asleep right there in her belly.

Pa-pa said that when Mama entered this world on a cold winter day in December, it was nothing short of a miracle. He said that it seemed like the more the devil was determined not to let Mama enter into this world, the more determined my mama was to get here. So much so that she was almost born on the side of Interstate 10 when he and Me-ma had slid off the road after hitting a patch of black ice. That happened only after both had to shovel at least a foot of snow from the drive way and around the truck. Then, the windshield wipers stopped working, and the defroster gave out. Thanks to the ambulance heading back to the hospital after responding to a prank call, Me-ma and Pa-pa were picked up just in time for Me-ma to deliver their nine pound sixteen ounce baby girl in the emergency room waiting area. When Mama made up her mind, nobody could change it, not even the devil himself. Pa-pa said that my Mama's birth was the beginning of the war the devil waged on her life.

Tilda Laraine was an energetic, rambunctious little girl. There was not anything she thought she could not do. Her older sister loved her to pieces, but she had to admit that even though she was six years older than Tildy, as she was lovingly referred to by her family and friends; she couldn't do a thing with my mama. She truly danced to her own melody. Mama loved, as a young child, to make her family laugh. She would always beg her daddy to turn on one of their favorite dance shows, such as Soul Train or Solid Gold so that she could put on a show for her family. Me-ma would say, "That Tildy can dance better than she walks!"

The love she had for her family didn't change as Mama began to get older. The more babies her mama had, the more protective my Mama became. She would fight lions, tigers, and bears for her family. Even though my Pa-pa once stood straight up and measured a tall six feet five inches and weighed a solid two hundred ninety-five pounds, Mama was just as protective of him as she was her mother and sisters. She fought more men and boys than any good Christian girl should ever come into contact with especially being as beautiful as people couldn't help but notice. Me-ma noticed too and it scared her more than she ever let on.

Me-ma saw how people, especially of the male gender, paid attention to her daughter. Even though my Mama was as tom-boyish as they could come, she knew that one day her Tildy would also realize how beautiful she truly was. Me-ma would never know just how long that was going to take. There were other things that only Me-ma seemed to notice about my mama, too.

One day on Mama's eighth birthday, which happened to be December 24, 1975, Me-ma needed her to come help in the kitchen. Me-ma thought Mama was trying to avoid cooking and cleaning with her, her aunts, and Elsie, her oldest sister.

"Tildy! Tildy, I know you somewhere hiding little girl. Get yo'self down here and help in this here kitchen!" Me-ma called. Still there was no answer from the bedroom that Mama shared with her sisters. Marching down the hall and not finding her in the one bathroom that everyone shared, Me-ma burst in her daughter's' bedroom. There she found my mama sitting cross-legged on the floor, staring out the window as if someone was sitting there. Mama never moved, and Me-ma knew it was because she never heard her enter.

In Mama's lap was Me-ma's old worn leather Bible. Not understanding what she was seeing, Me-ma didn't move a muscle and tried to hold her breath for fear of interrupting something much bigger than what was going on in the kitchen. She watched her eight -year- old daughter nod her head to symbolize her understanding as tears flooded her little face, but not one sound came from her Tildy.

Me-ma closed her eyes for what seemed like only a second to thank the Lord for whatever it was she was witnessing because she knew He had to be in the midst of it; she would question that later in life.

Me-ma suddenly felt a slight brush against her arm and opened her eyes just in time to see Mama walk past her through the door out to the hall.

"Tildy", she called ever so softly.

"Yes, ma'am?"

Me-ma turned to the place where she had found her daughter listening to a voice she could not hear from a person she could not see. Her Bible was lying in the very spot my mama had been sitting.

"Tildy, what were you doing with my Bible? You know you not supposed to be playing church and most definitely not with my Bible."

"I wasn't playing, Mama."

With that, Me-ma watched as her Tildy walked slowly down the hall into the kitchen. They never spoke of the scene that Me-ma had encountered until much, much later.

<u>Chapter 2</u>

A Calling Answered

And he said unto them, Go ye into all the world, and preach the gospel to every creature. Mark 16:15

*E*arly one bright Sunday morning, Me-ma and Pa-pa woke up their girls and proceeded to prepare for church as they did every other Sunday. Upon their arrival, all the girls except my mama of course headed to youth church in the classroom adjacent to the main sanctuary of the church as they were expected.

"Tildy, you betta come on here before we all get in trouble for being late!" yelled Elsie, attempting to take charge as she always did when Me-ma wasn't around.

Me-ma wasted no time getting out of the car so she could report to the choir room to warm up the choir before service. She took her calling as the minister of music very seriously and refused to be embarrassed by off-key vocals.

Without skipping a beat or pretending that she might be even a little intimidated by her father's presence, Mama simply said, "I'm not going to youth church today. I got something else to do."

"What are you talking about, Tilda Larain Mitchell? Don't you go starting no mess and get yo' mama all worked up today."

Daddy only called her by her full name when he was serious, and knew Tildy really was up to something. "Girl, do you hear me?"

"Daddy, this is the Lord's business, and I

must be about my Father's business."

Mama left her daddy sitting right there in the front seat of his prized 1963 Cadillac Seville with his mouth opened wide enough to catch a frog and his eyes so big he looked like a fly. Mama carefully smoothed down her dress, which she despised as she did all dresses, and she walked in the front door of the main sanctuary.

Right as she entered, Sis. Inew, the biggest gossiper in all of Arkansas, grabbed Mama's arm a little tighter than she would have any other child. Truth be told, she didn't care too much for my mama, and Mama didn't care at all for her.

Jerking away, Mama glared at Sis. Inew with a look that could have stopped the devil. Mama continued right up the aisle until she reached the very front pew and took her seat.

Whispers could be heard all over the church, just like she was told there would be, but her mother sat still as a statue and just watched her not knowing what was to come.

As Pastor Hewman brought one of his fire and brimstone sermons to a close, and Sis. Inew got happy at the door and worked her way up the aisle. She never missed a Sunday. Mama knew it was time. She stood up and walked right up to the very spot where she knew Sis. Inew always fell down after being slain by the Holy Spirit (or thrown down by some kind of spirit). Sis. Inew's praises suddenly stopped, and she glared at mama with fire in her eyes but said not a word.

This was one of the many times my mama would confront the buffoonery of those within Holy Ghost Fulfillment Baptist Church. Mama didn't even acknowledge the chairs Sis. Wright and Bro. Upmost brought up to the altar when the Pastor gave the invitation for the saved to come and accept Christ into their lives as their Savior. Mama stood confidently and ready to speak.

The thing was, Mama was already

saved and had been since she was six, and she had been baptized at the time as well. As far as Mama was concerned, she was here on business, her Father's business.

Since she was the only member to come forth, Pastor Hewman came from the pulpit and asked why she had come.

"Pastor, giving honor to the One and Only True God, my Lord and Savior Jesus the Christ, and the Holy Spirit, I come to let you, with all due respect, my family, and fellow sisters and brothers know that I have received my calling."

You could have heard a rat pee on the carpet. It seemed like everyone in attendance that Sunday was frozen in time.

Pastor Hewman replied, "Hallelujah! Glory to God! And a child shall lead them!"

Little did he realize that this child was being

led by a Higher Power much stronger than him, and he would remember his words upon his dying day.

After service, Pastor Hewman had Deacon Dewright summon the Mitchells and their Tildy to the pastor's study.

"Good afternoon, Mitchells. Please come in and take a seat. God is good and has saw fit to bless you all with favor! It ain't every day that he raises up a child to preach His Word, a young girl at that! This is truly a gloriously blessed day! Amen?"

Pa-pa was still shell-shocked concerning his daughter's bold statement just ten minutes ago and could only mumble, "Amen."

Me-ma was no longer surprised. She had realized at the moment of Tildy's confession that her child was as real as she had ever seen them come. At that moment, everything from the trying time of labor with Tildy to the scene she dared not mention to anyone, not even to Tildy, made sense. Tilda Larain, her second daughter, her baby, had indeed been called by the Lord, and Me-ma had been allowed to see it with her very own eyes. Me-ma hoped the pastor understood fully that he was dealing with one of God's anointed and asked him about this directly.

Me-ma spoke quietly, but firmly, "Pastor, I confirm that my child is telling the God's honest truth. My question is not whether or not Tilda can handle what God has called her to do. My concern is whether or not YOU can handle what God has called Tilda to do. Well, Pastor, can you? Can you handle one whom God, Himself, has raised up? You say so all the time that it is dangerous to play with God's anointed."

"Now, Sister, I have been carrying the Gospel to and fro for over 20 years now. Trust and believe I know how to handle this situation.", laughed Pastor Hewman, but he sounded a little agitated at Me-ma's direct questioning.

"Well, Pastor, what happens next?"

Pa-pa couldn't help but be a little skeptical about this. Not only was Tilda a tender eight, soon to be nine, years old, she was also a little GIRL. Who would take her seriously? Pa-pa didn't even know if he believed Tildy being he had never even seen her pick up a Bible.

"Brother Mitchell, let me assure you that I will personally take Tilda Larain under my wing. I will train her and protect her. I will meet with Sister Tilda every Saturday afternoon and allow her to shadow me on Sundays. If this is God's will, then I am grateful to be at service to Him in this capacity and will treat Sister Tilda like the blessing she truly is and has been to you all."

Pastor Hewman sounded convincing to my grandparents that day, and before they left they were comforted and at peace with the path that Tildy had chosen. Tildy had chosen to obey the Lord and preach His Word so they thought. My grandparents knew that all they could do was love and pray her through. The funny thing is no one ever asked my mama about her calling or how she felt about it. As a matter of fact, no one even asked my mama what she was called to do; they just assumed that Tilda's calling to minister would be like everyone else's had been. They would realize much too late that they were all tragically mistaken.

<u>Chapter 3</u>

An Innocence Stolen

God is our refuge and strength, an ever-present help in trouble.
Psalm 46:1

*M*ama had been preaching, teaching, and praying in her home church and around the surrounding counties for three years. She had just turned eleven, and she felt herself changing in so many ways. She had grown spiritually, mentally, emotionally, and physically.

Mama's physical beauty could not be denied; she was an amazing sight to partake. Her dark hair that fell down past her shoulder, if left down and not pulled back in a ponytail, highlighted her dark features and brought out her beautiful brown eyes. She had become taller over the summer and was now standing 5'2. She was shapely even at eleven and knew the boys in her school were greatly intimidated, but she hated the way some grown men looked at her, even in the church. When Mama was allowed to teach Sunday School and Bible Study her eyes lit up and you could hear, see, and feel her passion for God's Word. When Mama preached, you felt fire from deep down within your bones as the prophet Jeremiah said.

She took her ministry where ever she was allowed, but Pastor Hewman would not allow her to go anywhere without him. Mama had begun to feel uncomfortable around him, but dared not speak this about the pastor for fear that God would not be pleased.

One Saturday, as she always did, Tilda entered the church for her pastoral training with Pastor Hewman. Usually, it was quiet and peaceful when she arrived, and Pastor Hewman would be waiting for her in the sanctuary.

Today, however, music was coming from the church radio and was oddly loud, she noticed. Pastor Hewman appeared in the doorway that led to the Pastor's Study.

"Hi, Tilly, we are going to work back in my study today."

With that, Pastor Hewman turned and went back into the study. Mama hated the nickname he had taken upon himself to give her, but knew better than to sass the man of God. She wondered where Sis. Good was today. Sis. Good was a faithful member and committed to taking care of the House of Prayer, but today, Mama figured, she wasn't going to show up.

Mama reluctantly made her way to the pastor's study, but didn't see the pastor until he had shut the door behind her. Even though he did so quickly, my mama noticed he had locked the door.

"Tilly, we need to discuss something very important. Come sit on the couch with me."

Mama noticed that the pastor didn't have on his ministerial collar today. As they sat on the sofa, Pastor Hewman placed his hand on Mama's knee. Mama quickly slid over and away, but realized she was at the end and there was nowhere to go.

"It's okay, Tilly. Today's lesson is about honoring your leadership. You know that is very important to God that His people honor those whom He has set as leaders before them. I'm going to teach you how you can honor me like only someone of your anointing can."

Pastor Hewman began to rub up and down Mama's thigh and the more he did so the stranger he began to look and the more fragmented his breathing became.

"Please stop touching me, Pastor. It doesn't feel right to me," Mama said in a firm, but respectful tone. "Tilly, it feels different because no one has loved you like I do. It feels strange because this is new, but you will appreciate the lesson I'm teaching you when you begin to understand how strong this love is between God's chosen."

Grabbing her by both her hips and pulling her to the carpeted floor, Pastor Hewman pinned my mama down.

"NO! Please, Pastor, don't do this!"

Knowing no one was in or near the church that would hear my mama's desperate cries, Pastor Hewman saw no reason to attempt to make my mama stop screaming. He never raised his voice above a whisper."

"Tilly, please try to relax and let me love you. Let me teach you about an amazing love that no one else will be able to show you. I know you love me because of the way you watch me in the pulpit. This will just bring us closer."

"NO, NO, NO! NO, Pastor, it's not like that love. Please, please, please DON'T DO THIS!"

Tired of fighting, Mama now lay there half naked under a man she thought she could trust, a man who had promised her parents to teach and PROTECT her. Mama stopped fighting. She felt the physical pain of what was taking place, but the spiritual damage had been done the moment he touched her. As the pastor of the church that my mama had always loved raped her for what seemed like an eternity, my mama remembered what God had told her in her room on her eighth birthday.

"Daughter, the journey that is in front of you will not be an easy one. You will experience pain, loss, and suffering, but the seed that you will bear will be a great work, and I will be with you until the end. Your story will be told; your testimony will be given; though they will pretend they aren't listening, people will hear you and remember their sins. They will repent and know that I am God. Will you accept what is your purpose?"" That day as she cried, she put all of her trust and hope in Him, and told Him "yes."

"Now, Tilly, get up and go clean yourself up real good."

As he stood over her, sweating and panting like an animal, Pastor Hewman stretched out his hand to offer her help in lifting her aching body off of the now blood stained floor. My mama crawled to the bathroom with her undergarments looped around one foot. She stayed there until the Pastor, panicking that she had passed out, began beating on the door.

"Tilly! Tilly! Tilly, are you okay? Come out of there, right now! It's getting dark child, and you best be getting home."

Emerging from the bathroom, she walked right past him, as though he were air, and out of the door. Before exiting, she did notice that where her blood had stained the carpet was now a wet spot partially covered by what appeared to be a new throw rug. The good pastor must have been cleaning up the evidence of his sin, while in the bathroom, she tried to talk her mind out what had just happened to her.

My mama never looked back, knowing she would never see the inside of that place again. Having memorized Luke 9:62, concerning the gospel plow, my mama left feeling she was no longer fit for the kingdom because, come hell or high water, she was never going back. Mama entered into her home through the kitchen. She heard loud voices coming from the family room, and it sounded like her mother was crying.

"Something's wrong!" cried Me-ma."

"Just try to stay calm, y'all. If Tildy ain't home in the next five minutes, I'll go out looking for her. She's probably somewhere hemming up some teasing boy and has lost track of time."

Pa-pa did not even sound like he believed that.

"Tildy, takes her calling too seriously and wouldn't make us worry like this. I'm going with you to look for her." Though she didn't voice it much, Elsie's love was evident in her tone.

"He hurt me."

It was all my young violated mama could get out. She had cried the three miles from the church aloud, and now, her throat was sore.

"Oh, TILDY! Where have you been? What did you say?" her mama asked in a mixture of joy and anger.

"Who hurt you, Tildy?"," June and August asked, almost in perfect unison, as if they were the only two who had heard my mama's statement.

Belle, her beautiful baby sister, was sitting on the floor by my mama's feet. She reached out and touched Mama's foot."

"Tildy, you bleeding!"

"WHAT?" Mama yelled.

Everyone, including Mama, who didn't realize she had started back bleeding as she walked home, looked down at her legs. Sure enough, dark red blood flowed down her inner leg. At that moment, something took over my mama. She let out a sound at the top of her lungs that was equivalent to a wild animal in severe pain and with every ounce of strength that was left in her eleven-year-old body, she screamed,

"HE HURT ME!"

Tamara S. La Guins

Having no strength left, she passed out leaving her family afraid, shocked, and confused.

Chapter 4

A Broken Heart & A Damaged Soul

The LORD is close to the brokenhearted and saves those who are crushed in spirit.
Psalm 34:18

*T*here was no doubt that my mother had been raped, but by whom remained a mystery, or rather a secret that no one dare spoke of or made suspicions about except my mama. She refused to deny Hewman, as she called him from that horrendous day forward, raped her. Mama's family had a harder time than she accepting this fact. While they continued to support the man behind the book board, mama stopped attending church and stopped doing anything that had to do with the good churchfolks.

Mama stopped preaching and even stopped going out of the house altogether.

She even stopped talking when she realized no one was going to even entertain thoughts of a preacher, their beloved pastor, raping a child, let alone an anointed child. Her sister Belle, a lot like Mama, said she overheard one of the busty pastoral groupies refer to Mama as "that lying fast tailed young'un."

As her belly began to stretch and her body began to accept the growth within, my Mama stayed in her room under the covers. She wasn't ashamed of my conception because I was evidence that the pastor had been there, however she did not want to fight rumors and condemning stares everyday.

One day, at about seven months pregnant, believing she was the only one still awake, Mama could not control her craving for buttermilk any longer and headed to the kitchen. She walked straight into her father.

Looking at her as though she were the serpent from Eden's garden, Pa-pa, barely whispered her name,

"Tildy?"

He slowly reached out and touched the huge bulge held tightly within the nightgown she had stolen from Me-ma's drawer. Tears ran down his face as he fell to his knees. Fearing something terrible was happening to her father, for she had not seen this giant of a man react like this before, she screamed for her mother to come quickly. The entire clan of Mitchell women ran into the family room.

They all caught their breath upon sight of Pa-pa on his knees in front of the very pregnant Tildy. Feelings of betrayal by those whom she loved most overwhelmed her, and Mama began throwing every insult she could to protect herself from their stares and the impending danger she felt was near. Tears began to flow from her own eyes as she tried with all her might to push her father away from her, but exhaustion took over, and she reluctantly fell into his arms. Believing it now safe to come near her, her mother and sisters slowly went to where Mama stood in Pa-pa's embrace.

One by one, they joined in wrapping their arms around this beloved child with a broken heart, damaged soul, and pain in her eyes. Alas, Me- ma broke the silence and sent the other girls back to bed. As if communicating with her own baby telepathically, she led my mama to the kitchen table, with her husband right behind them, and then fixed Mama a big glass of ice cold buttermilk.

Smiling at her baby and running her fingers

through Mama's thickening hair, Me-ma told Papa she would take care of Mama and to go back to bed. Once he was gone, Me-ma took her coat from the coat closet and put on her scarf. She asked Tilda Lorain if she could see herself back to bed. Nodding affirmation, my mama watched her mother open a drawer in a nearby china case. She pulled out a pistol Mama had certainly never seen before and placed it in her purse that hung on one of the chairs sitting around the table.

Without looking her way, Me-ma said, "Goodnight, daughter. You will sleep well tonight," and walked out of the front door into the black of night.

Too afraid to go after her mother, Mama went to her room and climbed into bed without making a sound. Trying to make sense out of what she had just witnessed, Mama soon fell asleep. She was awakened the next morning by smells of thick smoked bacon, eggs, and biscuits only her mama could make. Entering the kitchen, her family was already up and getting set for breakfast.

"Morning, baby girl, come sit down," her father instructed.

After leading them in prayer, Me-ma made a startling announcement.

"Pa, you will need to refill the tank this morning; it's about empty."

No one knew or questioned why or how Me-ma would come to this conclusion because everyone knew Me-ma never drove. With the family left bewildered, Me-ma began humming and eating as if it were any other day. Suddenly there was a loud urgent knock at the door.

Not missing a beat, Me-ma continued to enjoy the fruits of her labor, and Pa-pa, jolted back to reality at the sound of his name being called, went to see what all the fuss was about. Pa-pa returned to the table with a stunned face as if someone had drained the blood from his body. The case was serious because Pa-pa rarely referred to Me-ma by her name.

"Rebekah."

Me-ma responded without looking up and continuing to eat, "Yes, Isaac?"

"Rebekah, someone shot the pastor dead last night in his home."

"Now, that is a shame, Isaac," as she continued to savor every lady-like bite of her breakfast, "I'm sure he will be missed."

"Rebekah, they found him in his study with his pants and underclothes around his ankles."

Me-ma finished the very last bite of her meal, gently placed her fork across her plate, dabbed the corners of her mouth with her napkin before placing it, too, on her plate, and then slowly faced Pa-pa.

"Well...... I guess that makes it his shame then." My mother watched her father walk over to the same drawer she had just hours before seen her mother pull a pistol from, but he couldn't seem to find what he was looking for as he rambled and almost pulled out the entire drawer.

Dropping his head, he ever so carefully turned to Me-Ma who had watched his every move, and calmly said,

"I'm going to refill the tank, Rebekah. I forgot I stopped by Bull's the other day after work."

"Yes, sweetheart, you should do that. You look like you could use the fresh air."

Three months, two weeks, and a day later, I entered the world. It was said that I came screaming with hands open and arms flailing, as if I was reaching out for rescue, but when placed in my mother's arms, I immediately calmed. It was then my mother being only twelve years old spoke over me,

"You were conceived in wickedness, but will defeat evil righteously."

"Tilda", Me-ma spoke as she held me in her arms for the first time, "there is no mistaken who her father is.

"Are you going to tell her my sin?"

"Your sin is your business, Ma. I'm going to love her with the love that's left in me."

That was as close to a confession as my grandmother ever came to confessing her deed to another human being. What was not said between mother and daughter on the day of my birth was well understood. Pastor Hewman was my father, and my grandmother made him give his life for that.

My mother never questioned her mother's love for her again, but the damage had been done. The seed of pain had been birthed, and my mother couldn't let it go.

<u>Chapter 5</u>

Bitter Is Her Name

"Do not bear a grudge against others, but settle your differences with them, so that you will not commit a sin because of them. Do not take revenge. .."
Leviticus 19:17-18

*A*fter my birth, Mama officially traded her Bible for a bottle (her own, not mine). By thirteen, she was a full-fledged alcoholic, and she was very promiscuous. It was her way of literally drowning out the scenes of her trauma and trying to satisfy an ache that never went away. Me-ma and Pa- pa never knew how she got it, the alcohol or the men, but the guilt that had a hold on them refused to let them question any of Mama's actions. Carrying and birthing a baby by a man whom had broken her with his lust and greed did more than just change Mama's mind; her body had curves where she had not noticed them before. She knew that if a so-called godly man could lust for a young girl, she could use this new vessel to cause men to do the unspeakable. Mama was set that every man should suffer for her internal pain and she was hell-bent and hell-bound to make that happen. Yes, my beautiful mother couldn't move past her pain to see God was still there. She couldn't push past the hurt to feel the Lord's warm embrace. The town was about to be reckoned with by this beautiful, broken, bitter woman.

At thirteen, Mama went where she wanted, when she wanted, and with whom she wanted.

"Where are you going, Tildy? 'Cause I ain't babysitting no baby."

"I don't recall asking you too, Elsie." Elsie knew when to back off.

"Well, where is she going to go while you laying on your back?"

"Big sister, it is in your best interest to concern yourself with your own back and let me handle my child and mine."

It wasn't so much of what Mama said that caused people to think twice about what they were saying or what they wanted to say to her, but it was more of how she said things. Glaring at Elsie with raised eyebrows and a slight smirk that hinted of danger, Mama made it clear that Elsie should never question her actions again.

Mama had taken me with her wherever she went. When she stepped into Bull's Juke Joint, I was holding her hand. Oh, the stares and whispers, but no one dared question this girl. As I became older, I realized my grandparents were not the only ones who possessed a great amount of guilt.

Those that never saw fit to turn my mother away were either gripped by guilt, thought she was crazy, or were sleeping with her. People couldn't get past their own emotions to see my mother for the child she still was.

As she thought, no one cared about her burden.By the time Mama was twenty-one, we had our own place about two miles away from Pa-pa and Me-Ma. Me-ma was furious with Mama for taking me and moving out.

Pa-pa kept asking, "How are you going to take care of the both of ya?"

Me-ma knew. Mama didn't have a job and didn't ever plan on getting one. Me-ma knew Fly Jesse, the town nickname for Mr. Jesse Banks, was footing the bill on Mama's new three-bedroom house and the gold Cadillac she drove. It could have been, Me-ma thought that Mama was just too beautiful and gifted to settle for the likes of Fly Jesse, who was known around town to be *the* ladies' man, but more than likely, it was his wife and his pregnant mistress that Me-ma had a difficult time accepting.

Mama wasn't worried and didn't care about either woman.

Fly Jesse wasn't a man in her eyes; he was whatever he was good for at the time of her needing or wanting.

"Carrington, come brush your Mama's hair."

Only Mama referred to me by my full first name, everyone else called me "Caring."

"What do you think about Mr. Jesse?" I didn't know what she wanted me to say, but I knew she expected to hear the truth. One thing Mama raised me to do was speak up and don't sugar coat.

"I think Fly...I mean Mr. Jesse is handsome for his age."

"Girl, what you know about MR. Jesse's age?" Mama giggled.

"I heard Me-ma fussing and telling Pa- pa that MR. Fly Jesse was 30 years older than you." I had a slick mouth, too. "So that makes him about 51, right, Mama?"

"How you get to be so smart? Must get that from your Me-ma." Mama laughed aloud. "Mama, what you want with a man that old?" Even at my young age, I knew I never had to fear my mother's rage. She always looked at me with love in her eyes despite my father's sin.

"Baby, Mr. JESSE is not a man. He is someone that plays on emotions and preys on the heart. So, I treat Mr. Jesse the way he wants to be treated."

That was so true. Fly Jesse cussed at his wife and made her cry. He fussed at his mistress and made her cry. But when it came to my mama, he did the crying, the begging, and the spending; Mama did the playing. The more he spent and begged, the more Mama acted like she could care less if he came by or not. It was truly a sight to see the man who everybody wanted acting like a fool when he saw my momma even spit towards another man. Fly Jesse wasn't the first man Mama lit a fire inside, and he wouldn't be the last. Everybody knows that fire isn't meant to be played with. It burns out if not maintained and destroys if left uncontrolled.

One night while Mama was entertaining new company, Fly Jesse came skidding into our driveway on two tires. He jumped out of his own emerald green Caddie, screaming Mama's name in a drunken rage.

Before Fly Jesse came crying and cursing in our yard, his wife and mistress, finally fed up with his whorish ways and his spoiling Mama, decided to confront him. The women marched right into Bull's and demanded Fly Jesse to choose between the two of them and to leave Mama alone altogether. Even though he had three children with his wife and two, now, with his mistress, Fly Jesse laughed in their faces like they were the funniest jokes he had ever heard.

"If you two sorry wenches think for a second that I'm going to give up my prize possession for either of you, you might as well pack up my clothes at yo' house and yo' house and take them to her house RET now!" But they were ready for his harsh words this time. His mistress, who looked like she may have been carrying again, smiled mischievously at his wife.

"Sounds like this fool believes that tramp belongs to only him." And she laughed just as coldly as Fly Jesse. Fly Jesse's wife responded as if on cue, "Well, husband, you might want to go tell that gentleman that has her calling on the good Lord tonight to unhand your prize possession or at least handle it with a little more care. I didn't see him go in with a Bible so I don't believe he's witnessing to her, but she certainly is shouting!" Leaving Fly Jesse with his mouth almost touching his wing-tips, the ladies turned and strutted out with a bit more confidence than when they entered.

"Tilda Larain!!!"

I sat on the steps of our porch watching this drunken man slur my mama's name and fall all over the yard.

"Tilda Larain! Get out here, Woman!   And bring that dead man wit'cha!"

Slowly, my mother appeared in the doorway of our home. The home Fly Jesse had paid off. She was draped in a sheet that showed the silhouette of her beautiful body; only her shoulders, calves, and feet left uncovered. Her long black hair was left down and draped over one shoulder. She was unfazed at the sight of this crazed man in her yard.

Sarcastically, Mama answered his crying.

"Really? Jesse don't you see I have company?"

"Baby, why you doing this?"

"What am I doing, Jesse?"

"Woman, don't play wit me? You know I love you."

"Aren't you the player?"

"Tilda, Baby, I love you."

"There was never an us. Fly away, Fly Jesse."

"Send him out, Tilda. You're mine. I'll kill the man that touches you."

Fly Jesse pulled out a gun and pointed towards the door as he staggered and struggled to aim where he thought the mystery man would come from, but he never saw it coming. Mama's company must have come from the back of the house and crept around Fly Jesse's car as Mama distracted him. Because suddenly, he was behind Fly Jesse, grabbing him in some type of choke hold as if he was trying squeeze the gun from Fly's hand.

Jesse broke free and spun around. Both men begin to battle for possession of the gun. Mama grabbed my arm and pulled me back into the house. She calmly told me to sit on the floor and stay away from the door. She picked up the phone and gave the person on the other end our address.

"Yes, there's been ………." One solitary gunshot pierced through the night and left us surrounded in a suffocating silence.

"A shooting."

She hung up, and went to her cupboard. After pouring herself a shot of Patron, she took her glass and sat on the sofa beside my spot on the floor, still draped in her sheet which smelled like lavender.

"Baby Girl, go get the brush and brush your mama's hair."

The police in our town didn't ask any questions. Things were still tense between the races in Midtown so one less black male didn't sound an alarm. They came with the coroner who picked Fly Jesse's body up from our yard and slapped handcuffs on the mystery man. Mama was never even questioned and never even went back to the door. About three days later, hand in hand, Mama and I walked to the graveside ceremony for Fly Jesse. Not waiting until the preacher was done or asking anyone's permission, Mama walked right up to the casket of her lover and placed a deep blood red rose on top of it. There were many hostile glares, but no one, not even his wife and certainly not his mistress, spoke a word of indignation to her.

"See, Baby Girl, always remember. You are a woman; that's power."

Chapter 6

One Sin-Every Man's Demise

"Be angry, yet do not sin. Do not let the sun set while you are still angry, and do not give the Devil an opportunity to work."
Ephesians 4:26-27

Mama was powerful. At least whatever she did to the men that entered her life was powerful. It's like she was a female spider that mated and then killed the male spider; a Black Widow. Except Mama didn't exactly kill these men with her own hands. It's more like she hooked them and then left them in a withdrawal like state. Some eventually disappeared as quietly as they came.

Others seemed to lose their minds and take out their frustrations with Mama out on their wives or girlfriends. They destroyed themselves. Once, I asked Mama did she feel bad about what she did to these men, and her response was strange to me at the time.

"Mama, don't you feel bad about how people calling you home-wrecker or "Black Widow?"

To my surprise, she chuckled.

"And why would I feel bad about being on everybody's simple little minds, Dearie?"

"Mama, I hate the way they say you don't care about anybody. I know that's not true. You care about me."

Mama ran her fingers through my hair and pulled me close to her.
"Baby, don't let hate change your heart.

I'm not doing anything to these men that they wouldn't do to me or that hasn't already been done. There is a wrong that has not been made right, and well, hell has no fury like me."   It was times like this that Mama couldn't hide   the pain that crept into her beautiful dark eyes. Times like these, I could tell Mama was struggling with some dark pain that she refused to let go   of and heal.

"Mama, I read in the Bible that if you want God to forgive you for your sins, that you have to forgive those that have sinned against you."

"Baby, I haven't asked God to forgive me. I'm simply helping God like He didn't help me."

And there it was. My mother wanted every man to hurt for something she dared not talk about, but it was something that still caused her great pain. My heart broke for her, but most of all, I feared for my mother's poor soul. I knew that she couldn't go on like this, and I was nowhere near ready to lose her.

"Mama, aren't you afraid of going to Hell?"

She stood up from the sofa we cuddled on late in the evenings and walked towards her bedroom. As her feet crossed the threshold, she turned slightly just so I could hear her.

"Well, you reap what you sow. That's the Word, but Baby, Mama entered hell a long time ago."

<u>Chapter 7</u>

What Goes Around Comes Back ....Heavy

Whoso diggeth a pit shall fall therein: and he that rolleth a stone, it will return upon him.
Proverbs 26:27

*M*ama was so taken off guard with this stranger who came riding through town in a shiny red 1973 Monte Carlo leaning back so much on the driver's side that from a distance you would have thought he was driving from the back seat. With one hand he gripped the cherry wood stirring wheel and bobbed his head as he kept the time of the rhythm with his neck.

When he saw that brown sugar complexion draped over those firm curves of Mama's, even I thought she had taken another mind captive so that she could play with his heart. His eyes followed the gentle swish and sway of Mama's hips as we came out of Mr. Mill's Market. I watched this daily reaction from yet another strange man. What I wasn't expecting was the same look of intensity on my mother's face that the stranger was still wearing. Without even putting the groceries into the car, Mama walked over to the passenger side of his car, got in, and shut the door as if she had known this man all her life. I'm not sure what the conversation was about, but when Mama got out of the car, she and Mister had big,goofy smiles on their faces.

"Mama, who is that and why he looking at you like that?

"Stay in your lane, Ms. C. Mama got this. That man is going to change our lives."

"But Mama, we don't know him do we?"

"Baby, I want that man, and I'm going to have him so you just play nice and mind your manners. You HEAR me?"

"Yes, ma'am."

I'm not sure what it was about Mr. Antwan Walton, but I am sure that I didn't like him. I don't know if it was his phony, high-pitched, "Hi Kid!", or his wide grin that seemed too big for his face. It could have been his beady, little eyes. Whatever it was gave me an ache deep down in the pit of my belly. I just somehow knew that he was not the man for my mama. I wouldn't know until it was too late just how true this thought would prove to be.

It didn't take long before Antwan was coming over to visit with Mama on a daily basis. Everyday around the same time, Antwan would come by in his work uniform and sit his feet under Mama's table like he was the king of the castle.

Mama wouldn't hesitate to fix him a plate piled high with her menu for the evening. MY MAMA!! I couldn't allow too much of my dislike for Antwan to show because he was the inspiration behind all the cooking Mama had started to do: Cabbage, collard greens, turnip greens, neck bones, pigs feet, homemade cornbread and biscuits, pork roast, black eye peas, macaroni from scratch you name it, Mama cooked it! It broke my heart, though, when I would watch Mama work like a slave in the kitchen all day to make sure everything was done and hot before Mister came through, only to realize by 8:30 pm, he wasn't coming.

"Ok, Sweet Girl, you go on and fix your food."

"Mama, I'll fix you a plate, too," would be my way of trying to convince her not to starve herself because Mister had disappointed her.

"Hush, now. Do what Mama tells you to."

I would try to eat more than usual and make

a big fuss about how good everything was to ease the pain of the sting that I know Mama felt.

"Baby, Mama not feeling too good. I'm going to take some headache tonic and go to bed. Love you."

Her headache tonic consisted of three consecutive shots of moonshine kept under her bed. Mama took her liquor the way she showed herself to be with people: straight, no chasers. She was an alcoholic, and everyone knew it. Even though she wasn't a sloppy drunk, she was an alcoholic just the same. I don't know how, but I could see Mama diving head first into her alcoholism the longer Mister filled her mind with fairytales of being a family and loving her. I don't even know how I knew he was lying, but I knew.

No matter what I knew, I dared not tell Mama, even as I watched her drink to get up, drink to get going, drink to calm down; and drink to sleep.

When Antwan was around, I had never

seen Mama smile brighter or laugh louder. She experienced a joy that I never knew existed in my mother, almost the kind of joy I saw come from within Me-Ma when I went to church with her. The confusing part was seeing this undefinable joy come from two strong-willed women and from two different sources. Me-ma described her's as everlasting and from out of this world. Mama would say that this man brought her so much joy that it seemed unreal. All I was sure of was that I wanted that kind of joy one day. I just didn't know quite yet from which source.

Mama didn't just serve up food either. Anytime Mister called, Mama was right there. Sometimes the ring of the phone would awaken both of us in the middle of the night with a gripping fear that it might be something wrong at Pa- pa and Me-Ma's. Running right behind her, we would race to the phone panting for air as Mama anxiously answered.

"Hey, Baby! What you doing? I know you ain't

sleep," Antwan's slurred speech could be heard despite Mama trying to cover the phone's speaker.

"Antwan, do you know what time it is? Where are you?" Mama could never hide the concern and relief that she had in her voice when he finally decided to call.

"I miss you, Baby. Don't you want to see, Big Daddy?"

His voice sickened me. He didn't care anything about Mama or me. It was ALL about Antwan Watson. Everyone else was expendable and replaceable. I don't even believe Mama realized it, but she had indeed met her match. Antwan Watson had come with a power my mother either couldn't compete with or had become addicted to perhaps both.

"You reap what you sow." Something told me that my mother had come into her harvest season.

<u>Chapter 8</u>

Change Gon' Come

"The Lord is not slow in keeping his promise, as some understand slowness. Instead he is patient with you, not wanting anyone to perish, but everyone to come to repentance."
II Peter 3:9

I watched for months as my mama allowed Mister to run crazy. Didn't see much of Mister until he was drunk and in a particularly touchy-feeling mood. He called when he needed money, food, or a ride from here to there. I watched as Mama constantly stared out of the window after he said he was on the way only to be sick with disappointment as day turned to dusk and the moon took the place of the sun.

That's when I begin to hear it: crying in the darkest part of the night. My mother was secretly falling apart. She smiled, laughed, and spoke as if life was a party when we had to go out, but under the covering of the darkness and behind the closed door of her bedroom, my mother was wasting away.

One night, as lay in my bed listening to Mama sobbing, it sounded as if she was talking to someone. I couldn't make out what she was saying, but I could understand one word she continued to cry out constantly, "DADDY." At first, I thought Mister was there, but when I went to the living room window to peep out, I saw he wasn't around. As a matter of fact, Mama and I had not seen nor heard from Mister in about two months, the longest he had ever been missing. This was strange, and it caused Mama a lot of pain.

I moved closer to her door to get a better

listen. I was so shocked at what I heard that I quickly scurried from the foot of Mama's door back to my own bed. Was my Mama really praying? I had never as so much heard her bless food, and now believing I was fast asleep she was praying as if God was sitting beside her at the kitchen table. Little did I know that my Mama was about to do exactly what my science teacher taught us about butterflies; she was about to undergo a metamorphosis.

After several weeks of listening to my mother's midnight or early morning prayers complete with a weeping that was enough to cause me to cry most of the time, I begin to notice drastic changes in my mother. Mama cleaned herself up one day and began working on all of the cleaning she had long forgotten. She started cooking for me again and was now even sitting down to eat dinner with me.

One day she even smiled as I told her about my day. I even noticed a worn out Bible on her nightstand one evening when I went in search of something in her room. Mama was reading Scripture? Even though she still refused to attend church with the family, I was comforted in knowing that Mama was receiving the Word.

It had been about four months since we last heard from Mister when suddenly there came a knock at the door. Me-maw had always said that if you talk or think on a person long enough, they are bound to show up. That's certainly what happened. Mr. Antwan Watson came a knocking one Saturday night as Mama and I were having our usual Saturday Night Spa Party.

It was almost as if she smelled him coming. We were in the middle of painting our toes when Mama suddenly looked toward the window and told me to go to my room. Just as I was pulling myself up from the floor, I saw Mister's car pulling into the driveway. I also saw that look in my Mama's eyes that I had not seen in a while, the look that sent chills up and down the spine and caused grown men to tremble. Needless to say, I was terrified to leave the room and even more terrified to be disobedient. I left the room, but I stood in the door of the bedroom so that I could hear what was going down. I knew something was about to go down.

"How can I help you, Antwan?"

"Heeeeeyyy, Baby! What's happening?"

It was obvious with his slurred, overly-excited speech that he was drunk. He probably couldn't get 'any' from some other woman so he made his way over to 'Easy Street.'

"How can I help you, Antwan? Please, don't touch me."

I wonder if he realized in his drunken stupor that love didn't live here anymore.

"Awww, come on, Baby. You not gon' let me
in?"

"No. I think you need to leave."

I could tell by her tone that Mama was not going to put up with much more of this. I heard the soft click of the safety being taken off of her ever-so-near pistol. I could also tell that she was hurting with every second that went by. She didn' t even wait for his response instead she closed the door and called my name.

When I entered the living room, I saw her leaning against the door. "Carrington, let's turn in. We have church in the morning," Mama quietly said to me. Without a word of dismay about going to bed early, I went back to my room in utter shock. Something was wrong, and I knew this was the quiet before the storm.

Chapter 9

With Change Comes Pain

"And not only so, but we glory in tribulations also: knowing that tribulation worketh patience"
Romans 5:3

*E*ven though my mother had begun to attend church service with the rest of the family regularly, it did not stop the cruel glares and audible snickering and gossip that circulated every time she walked in the door. What I couldn't understand is why my mother never said anything about it or even attempted to get some reckoning. She walked in the door with her head held high as if she knew she was royalty, and no one in the place had the authority to de-throne her.

She sat still and quiet amongst the dancing and shouts of praise throughout the congregation. She never opened her Bible, but I could see her mouthing every word of Scripture that came from the pulpit. My mother did not need a physical Bible in her hand. As the inspired writer of the Psalm 119:11 wrote of himself, she had "hid the word" in her heart so that she "would not sin" against God.   Mother was changing.

It seemed like sense my mom had turned Mister away she had received some sort of renewed strength. Not only had she dismissed Mister, but she was denying all the men who attempted to sweet talk her. She still did not spend much time with Me-ma or Pa-pa, and she certainly did not entertain friends, but she seemed at peace. My mother had never been at peace. Cool, calm, and collected, but never at peace.

"Mama, is everything okay with you?"

"Yes, Dearie. Why you asking such a thing?"

"Because, Mama. You going to church. You got this quiet spirit about you, and you ain't even said 'BOO' to a man. Let alone, let one in the house," I whined.

"Com' ere, Carrington," Mama spoke quietly. I just knew I was about to be smacked across the rear for stepping out of my lane, but too afraid to be disobedient, I prepared my body for the blow and went to her. To my surprise, Mama wrapped her strong arms around me and held me so closely that I smelled her vanilla mist and thought I would melt into her. I had to really strain to hear her. She spoke so softly, but her words sent shivers up and down my spine.

"Mama has made her peace with God, and her time is changing. I had to reap the harvest I planted. Now, sweet girl, it's a new season. Time to sow new seeds in better dirt."

As if right on cue, the phone startled both of us with a shrilling ring. We both stared at each other as we expected the other one to be able to provide some information about this late evening call. No one called our home except the usual telemarketer and bill collectors, and no one called after 9 o'clock. By the time Mama made a move to answer, it stopped ringing. Before we could exhale with relief another ring began, piercing the silence that had surrounded us. This time without hesitation, my mother answered the phone.

"Hello!" Mama answered a lot louder than she had intended. The look on her face is one I could never recall seeing before. A mixture of knowing and sadness filled my mother's entire face. Who was on the other end of the phone, I did not know. What I did know was that whatever it was being told to her was already having a profound effect on her.

"Carrington, your grandmother is calling for us. Put on your shoes and coat, and make haste." Doing exactly as she said, I returned to find my mother already outside in the cold. December had just arrived, and the season was indeed making itself known, but Mama had just grabbed her light jacket out of the coat closet by the door. She stood on the porch and appeared to be unfazed by the cold breeze that was blowing. As I locked the door, she began to descend the porch stairs. I hurriedly followed behind her and jumped in the car.

Mama did not speak a solitary word to me on the short ride to my grandparent's home. I did not know why we had been summoned over or what to expect when we arrived. I had just seen my mother's family on Sunday, and everyone seemed to be in good health and spirit. What could possibly be so urgent?

As we pulled into the driveway of my grandparent's home, Mama slowly cut the engine of the car, and without turning to me, she spoke.

"Carrington." She still spoke in the soft tone she had used at home when explaining this new attitude she was portraying.

"Your grandmother is transitioning and wants to make things right with you so that she can go home to God in peace".

Confused, I replied, "Mama, what is transitioning? I love Me-ma. There is no bad blood between us." As she explained "transitioning," I was not saddened by the announcement of my Me-ma's death. I understood that people are born and people die. I was more upset at the thought of Me-ma dying believing I was upset with her about something.

"Come on, child." Mother made no attempts to explain her statements, and answer my questions. I knew it was because of her belief that experience is one of the best teachers that mama stopped trying to explain what was about to happen.

When we entered the house, all of my aunts were sitting around the kitchen table. My Aunt

Elsie, without lifting her head from her hands told mama through her tears, "Tildy, she's been waiting on y'all. She wants both of you."

As we entered my grandparents' room, I began to understand why we were here. My grandmother was dying. A fool could tell that and she lay still and quiet as if she were practicing for her coffin. My grandfather's wide, tall frame looked wilted and small as he sat at the foot   of the bed with his shoulders slumped. He did   not even realize we had come in the room as   he held Me-ma's foot as if it were her hand.

"Daddy," Mama gently called to him.

Not even looking our way he told Me-ma, "Baby, the girls here." He stood up and went to the other side of the bed just for the second it took to grab hold of the other. I've never seen Pa-pa look so defeated and lost. Watching his best friend dying in the same bed that they had shared for what seemed an eternity must have been the most fearful he had ever been.

"Me-ma?"

She turned her head toward my voice and looked me right in the eyes.

"I love you, little girl. I'm so sorry that I took what I took from you, nothing ... compares to a mother's love or ... her rage. I hope you can find it in your heart to do what I believe God has done for me." She seemed to have spoken with all the energy she could.

"Forgive me."

"Me-ma, I do. I do. What's wrong? I love you. I could never stay mad at you," I whined with confusion.

"Mama, what is going on? Tell her it's okay", I demanded. My mother came closer and took her dying mother's hand.

"We love you, Mama, and We FOR – GIVE you." She stooped down and kissed her mother's forehead and whispered, "Go on home, and ask for mercy upon my soul."

As if she had been waiting for someone to release her by permission, my grandmother took her last breathe on what seemed to be my mother's que. My grandfather never turned around, but the shaking of the bed was enough to let us know that he was crying heavily. Mama and I left him alone with the love that had been his life.

Walking back through the living room and up to the table, my mother announced that their mother was gone. The wailing from the Mitchell Women could probably be heard at least a mile and a half away a wailing from the pain of losing one of their own; the pillar that had been used by the Creator to rear them up, protect them, teach them, and love them unconditionally. We were all hurting so deeply that even talking with each other was not consoling at the moment. Aunt June called 911 and explained what was happening. We all lost it as they removed Me-ma from the house.

As we all calmed our cries hours after Me-ma was taken away, I looked around at each of my aunts, Pa-pa, and my mother. They had a secret. They all seemed to know what Me-Ma had to get off her heart and ask forgiveness for, but no one was talking about it. My Me-ma was gone! She was my best friend, and she kept a secret from me. What else was my own family hiding? Later that night, I would find out more than I wanted to know. That secret would explain the void I had always felt, but it will never fill it.

<u>Chapter 10</u>

Where Is .... HE?

**"The LORD himself goes before you and
will be with you; he will never leave you nor
forsake you. Do not be afraid;
do not be discouraged"
Deuteronomy 31:8**

*A*rriving home, I thought we would
both continue on our separate ways to bed.
We did not speak in the car on the way back to
our home at all. The weight of my Me-Ma's death
was bearing on both of our hearts. I was taken by
surprise when Mama asked me to get prepared
for bed. Usually, she just said goodnight and went
to her room. I had no bedtime.

Confused, but not wanting to upset Mama any more than she already was, I hurriedly showered and dressed for bed. Coming from the hall bathroom, I heard the cries that I had often heard late in the night when I was expected to be asleep. This time, something was different. It sounded like Mama was having a conversation with someone in her room. Suddenly, I realized it was pouring outside and loud claps of thunder shook the windows of the bathroom. The more intense Mama's conversation became, the stronger the storm and the harder the wind blew; or so it seemed. The thunder became so loud that I had to move to the hall to hear the rest of the conversation.

"It wasn't supposed to be like this! NOT my Mama.

I'm tired. We have made our peace; I'm ready, but Mama was supposed to be here. My baby girl needs her. NOW what?" My sobbing mother sounded as if she was in more pain than she ever felt before. But, why? If she had made her peace with God, what had birthed this new pain? Was it new or was there more my mother wanted to escape from?

I saw the knob of her door slowly turning, and I scurried back behind the bathroom door. She exited her bedroom in a slow stupor. She walked as if she were in a drunken daze, but I could tell she was crying heavily. Watching her turn the corner, I followed quietly behind her. To my astonishment, she opened the front door and walked straight out into the storm. I followed as far as the door and started screaming for her to come back inside.

"Mama!! Mama, please, come back inside!"

She started screaming toward the sky, "You let him rape me, but I forgive. Please, forgive me! You let him take what was only mine to give, but I forgive! I forgive, DADDY! It hurts so badly, but I forgive! I forgive! Abba, set me free!" Suddenly, something I could not see came over Mama. She grabbed at her breast, and slowly, she dropped to her knees.

Time stopped for what seemed an eternity as I watched her fall face down in the grass. There was a sound like I had never heard before that pierced the dark, tumultuous sky. I learned later that the sound was my own scream- so loud and filled with fear and pain that it was heard a couple of blocks over.

I thought she had died in front of me, and she had. Emotionally exhausted, spiritually conflicted, and mentally confused, my mother became a shell. Dead inside.

I'm not sure how my Pa-pa knew of Mama's breakdown or how long she and I had been screaming in the ravenous storm, but he was the one who came and scooped Mama from the yard and me from the porch.

Mama had no fight in her as she allowed Papa to pick her up like a rag doll and place her in his truck. He gently coaxed me from the porch to the steps and lifted me. Looking into the frightened eyes of this gentle giant, I remember him saying, "It's gone be alright, Baby Girl."

Waking up in Mama's hospital room, I was a bit startled to find one of the nurses in front of me.

"Hello, Sleeping Beauty. Are you hungry?" She offered a plate of unappetizing food with a generous smile.

"No, thank you. Where's my mama?" I did not feel like returning her kindness; I needed my mama.

"Sweetie, your mama is speaking to one of our chaplains right now. She did not want to wake you so she asked if someone could look after you until they returned."

At that moment, Mama walked into the room followed by a man I had never seen before. He was shorter than Mama but handsome all the same. He offered me a small smile and concerned look for my Mama. This was new. The only look Mama ever seemed to get from men was a look that had them concerned with only one thing; her body. There was something different about this man.

As he pulled back the covers and tucked Mama into bed, his eyes never left her face.

"Please, get some rest Larain. I'll be back this evening to check on both of you."

"Thank you, Pastor, but you don't have to do that. My girl and I will be alright. We've been down before, but we always make it through."

"I know, but now, you won't have to do it alone. He sent me to you." With that, he kissed

Mama's forehead, and told me to rest, and he would be back with some real food for me when he returned. I noticed he wasn't wearing a wedding ring, so my muscles relaxed a bit.

He looked at Mama with a longing of some kind, but I was not sure of his intentions. Time would tell as always. Was he really God's answer to my mama's concern?

<u>Chapter 11</u>

Prayer Changes Things

"Whatever prayer or supplication is made by any man or by all Your people Israel, each knowing the affliction of his own heart, and spreading his hands toward this house; then hear in heaven Your dwelling place, and forgive and act and render to each according to all his ways, whose heart You know, for You alone know the hearts of all the sons of men."
I Kings 8:38-39

*O*ver the next few months, Mama stayed in the hospital. Diagnosed with severe depression, she left the general hospital for the mental hospital. To my surprise, she was not ashamed and told me that she was getting the help she knew she needed; she was tired of fighting an old ghost alone.

The mystery pastor, I learned, came to see her twice everyday, and he even stayed all day on Saturdays. My aunts, Pa-pa, and I often saw him when we visited Mama. He always stayed around and laughed and joked as if he were family too. I liked him, but I did not trust him. One day I mustered up the courage to ask Mama just who this man truly was and what did he want?

"Mama, who is Pastor?" I attempted to sound as innocent as possible for fear of her getting on to me about being in grown folks' business.

"Pastor?" She seemed genuinely confused at first.

"Ohhhhhh," she chuckled. "You talking about Pastor Luji. He is an old friend of your Pa-pa's. They grew up together, and he left home. He returned just a few years ago. Why, sweet girl?"

"I just never seen him before. He always saying he love you, but he don't even know you.

What does he want? Why is he always around, Mama?" I couldn't hide anymore. I was afraid for my mama.

I know she had done some things, but she was turning her life around and wasn't bothering anybody. I just wanted to see her well and happy finally happy.

"I know you worried about me, Carrington, but I'm much better than what I was. Pastor Luji is really close to your Pa-pa and this family. He loves me like a child of his own; that's all. We can trust him, Baby Girl."

Even though I trusted Mama, I was still not convinced. I knew the spell she put on men without even trying. I saw the captivated look clearer every time I saw Pastor Luji in her presence. Mama did not even realize that she was captivated, too.

"How are two of the most beautiful ladies I know doing today?" Pastor Luji entered the room, followed by Mama's counselor.

Mama's face lit up as soon as she laid eyes on him. "Well, aren't you especially happy today, sir?"

"I have some good news, and some bad news so which do you want first?"

"Give me the bad with salt or sugar," my mama joked backed.

"Ok, the bad news is that you don't have a choice in the matter that you are about to face."

Mama's smile disappeared and her strong jaw line tensed up as she spoke, "Ok, and the good news?"

"You are getting out of here today, and I am taking you home."

The brightness in her eyes returned as she hoped off the bed into his arms. She expressed her thanks to her counselor and listened to her release instructions adamantly as the pastor began to pack up her things. Did he just touch her panties? What kind of preacher was this?

I took my chance as Mama spoke with her counselor.

"Pastor Luji, are you married? My auntie says you married. If that's true, why you always coming to talk to Mama?"

He addressed my interrogation as he continued to pack up Mama's clean and unclean clothing.

"Technically, yes, I am still married. I am legally separated and in the middle of a divorce. I am sorry you had to hear about me the way that you have, but none of it has to do with you or your mama. Okay?"

I was surprised by his tone. He was not

harsh, but I did detect the sternness in his voice. I saw something in his eyes when he looked at Mama that I had never seen in any of the other men that came sniffing behind her.

Mama came back to the room ready to go home at last. The ride home with Pastor was quiet and uneventful, a change for Mama and me. Reaching the house, he helped Mama out of the car and into the house, handling her as if she were a fragile piece of china or a delicate flower. He told me she still needed rest, and he was counting on me to make sure she was not disturbed.

He left out but returned with food and a dozen yellow roses. He gave Mama the bouquet, but took one out and handed it to me.

"You are a part of someone special, a package deal."

I had never been given flowers before by anyone, and only my mama ever told me I was special. Over the next few months, Pastor would come by the house to check on Mama's progress and talk to me about how I was doing, school, and anything else I brought to his attention. He stayed until evening, sometimes, answering our questions about church, church folks, and the Bible. He told Mama He knew she had a calling but knew also the pain she used as wall to block people out. He always left saying, "The walls are coming down, Pastor, the walls are coming down."

One Sunday morning, Mama entered my room and announced we were going back to church. She seemed so excited that it was contagious. I hopped out of bed and hurriedly dressed for the day. To our surprise, Pastor Luji was already there talking with Pa-pa when we arrived. Oh, the murmuring when Mama walked into the church. The deacons were almost forgotten as heads turned to the cracked-up home wrecker entering on the arm of a preacher at that! Pastor seemed unfazed as he escorted Mama and me up the aisle to an empty pew.

He even sat with our family during services.

After service, for the first time since Me-ma had passed, we went to my grandparents' home where my aunts had prepared a feast! We ate, laughed, and reminisced about better times. We even prayed together about better days to come. Before leaving, Pastor and Mama walked outside. I peeked out the nearest window and saw them talking and walking around the yard. Before they turned to come back in, he wiped something from my mother's face, and they embraced for longer than usual. Shortly after they returned to the house, Mama and I packed some leftovers and went home. During the ride home, tears rolled down my mother's face, but she said not a word. Then, I heard my mother finally exhale.

SEASONS KEEP CHANGING
14 Years Later

<u>Chapter 12</u>
A Mother's Instincts

**"Plans fail for lack of counsel,
but with many advisers they succeed."
Proverbs 15:22**

So much time had passed us by. Pastor and Mama were the leaders of the very church Mama had always tried to avoid. Pa-pa had passed away peacefully at home in the very same bed in which Me-ma had slept away. All of my aunts were married and raising families, and I was the first college graduate of our family. Our change had indeed come, and I was so happy for my mother. To see a beautiful strong woman come through such pain and agony and embrace the same God that I always knew was there was a true blessing.

Perhaps it was watching my stepfather, or Pop, as I lovingly called him, operate in the church and deal with church folks, or the long talks he, my mother, and I had about spirituality, religion, and the Lord that caused me to follow the theological path. Whatever it was, God had allowed me to graduate from Libertine Seminary College with a Masters of Divinity. Mama and Pop even allowed me to speak on occasions at church and work with the young adults and youth. I could not complain about life; although, I could not help but wish Me-ma was here to be a part of it. I stilled missed her presence very much.

Sometimes my mind wandered back to the night she lay dying and begging my forgiveness for not protecting my mother. I dared not bring it up to my mother or aunts because they had moved past Me-ma's death, and I wanted to keep it that way. Still, the need to know this perpetrator, this monster, was sometimes overwhelming.

I was excited as another Sunday arrived. Pop had asked me to speak to the youth about the importance of loving themselves as God loves us. One of my professors, who had also been my mentor at Libertine Seminary, told me he would come and hear me. As we entered the parking lot, I spotted Professor Shaw standing next to his car speaking to one of the most beautiful creatures I had ever seen in this little town. The man was at least 6"1' and stood with a slim but athletic build. The type of physique with which so many in the NBA have been blessed. He was a dark chocolate and seemed to shine in the light of the sun. I had not even left the car, and I felt the weakness in my knees. I said a quick prayer for strength so my legs would not buckle when I exited the car and for self-control, so I would not salivate as I approached this drink of coffee.

"Pop and Mom, I see Professor Shaw has beaten us here, so I'll go over and walk him inside."

"Ok, bring him to the study and properly

introduce him to us, Baby." I knew Pop was not going to let me get away that quickly. I took my time approaching the two men so that I could stare at this piece of art a little longer. As I got closer, I noticed he sported a goatee, and he had the nerve to have good hair!!! I started praying harder.

"Excuse me, gentlemen." I was determined to play it cool and make him come to me. This meeting would determine just how much of mama I had within. Other than that fool Antwon, she had not chased a man.

"Carrington! It's so good to see you!," exclaimed Professor Shaw as he genuinely greeted me.

As we hugged, I spoke my good mornings to both men.

"If you both don't mind, I would like to escort you to the pastors' study to introduce you to the pastors of the church who happen to be my parents."

"I would be delighted," the gentleman spoke with a deep, sultry, baritone voice. It may have been my instantaneous physical attraction to him or my rising blood pressure, but his eyes seemed so familiar to me.

Professor Shaw and I caught up as we walked to my parents' study. He also introduced the young man, who looked to be just a little older than me, as James Reaper. James, it turned out, was only a few months older than I, and had been transferred to Libertine while I was a student. He was now a professor there, and Professor Shaw had become a close friend. He volunteered to journey with Professor Shaw to hear me speak. This made me even more nervous as it was about that time.

When we entered the study, it seemed as if the color briefly drained from my mother's face. "Mom?", I questioned.

She quickly regained her poise and greeted the professors with a timid "good morning."

"Mom and Pop, this is Professor Shaw, my mentor through seminary whom I speak of all the time, and this is Professor James Reaper, a friend of his and new professor at Libertine."

"Well, it is a pleasure to finally put a face with a name, Professor Shaw," Pop noted, "A pleasure to meet you, as well, Professor Reaper.

"It is indeed a honor to have two educators of the Word with us this morning, and we hope you enjoy our service today."

"You look so familiar, Professor. What is your name again? My mother spoke to Professor Reaper with a peculiar look on her face. It was strange that we both felt so familiar with this man.

Reaching out to shake her hand, he confidently introduced himself as James Reaper.

"Have you ever been to Midtown, Arkansas before, sir?" she casually asked.

"I passed through as a child, I was told," he replied to all of our surprise.

"Oh, do you have family in or near this area? It's such a small town. We may know some of your kin." Now, she just sounded like she was interrogating the man. I knew I better step in before this introduction made everyone uncomfortable.

"Mama, I should take them to find a seat. Service is about to start."

The Holy Spirit showed Himself in all during service. Even the professors seemed to be filled and free with their praise as the time approached for me to speak. I spoke briefly from the subject of having "A Constant and Consistent Friend." The Holy Spirit moved in and through me and continued to the spiritual momentum of the congregation.

After service, Professor Reaper expressed what a wonderful time he had with us. He said he knew he would not be disappointed with the

Word that would come from me and that he would definitely be in touch with me so he could hear me again. All the while he spoke, his eyes never left mine nor did he ever let go of my hand. When he did walk away as Professor Shaw and Pop approached, I saw my mother watching him and knew she had witnessed our brief but intense encounter. I knew this would soon be discussed.

As I knew, my mother brought up Professor Reaper at dinner.

"Carrington, have you seen James Reaper before while you were away at seminary"?

"No, mother, I don't remember ever meeting Professor Reaper before today. What is it about him that you don't like, Mom?" I tried to sound concerned rather than annoyed as I truly felt.

"I don't trust him. I know those eyes. I just can't seem to place them. He's not being completely honest. He has been here before, Carrington."

Pop decided to step in on this comment.

"Tildy, the young man admitted that during your interrogation. Why would he lie to us about anything? He doesn't know us."

Completely ignoring Pop's question, Mama came back to me, "Carrington, what did he say to you after service? I saw him run over to you."

"Mom, he just said he really enjoyed the entire service and would keep in touch so that he could hear me speak again." To end the conversation, I excused myself from the table and went to my room. As I walked past her, she tenderly grabbed my hand, "Carrington, be careful, my love."

I truly believed Mama was just being overprotective as she had always been. Kissing her forehead, I could not deny how much this woman loved me; even through her pain, her love for me was always evident. Lying on my bed, I remember how she cried like a baby when I announced that

I had been accepted into Libertine Seminary in Detroit, Michigan. She honestly expressed that she did not want me to go but admitted that she wanted me to do what was best for me. She cried everyday up until the day I departed. She called every day for the five years I was there. She arrived the day before my graduation day and spent the night in my dorm room with me to help me pack up all of my belongings, just so I could come straight home after graduation. Pop later told me that she cried every time I left after the holidays and on her birthday. My mother's love was not God's love, but it was a very close second.

Still, I was an adult and Professor was an adult, and what we chose to do about the seemingly mutual attraction was our adult business. Besides, I needed to stop telling my mother everything and truly grow up. I had to figure out how to see him again without coming across as desperate. As I worked my mind overtime trying to come up with a masterplan to see this man, my phone rang and startled me so that I bumped my head on the nightstand trying to answer it.

"Hello."

"Hi, Carrington, this is Professor Shaw. I just wanted to express how proud I am of you and how I see the Lord working in and through you. I also wanted to invite you to a seminar I am giving at the college on church planting, pastoring, and church growth. It's this weekend. I know it's last minute, but if you are not too busy, I think it's something you would enjoy and benefit from thoroughly."

"I am definitely interested in attending, Professor! What do I need to do?" This would be my chance to see him away from Mama's watchful eye.

"Nothing. You are my special guest. Professor Reaper has already volunteered to pick you up and take you back home safely. You can stay with my family in our guest quarters so do not concern yourself with lodging, food, or transportation."

"Oh, Professor, how do I ever thank you for such hospitality?"

He chuckled, "Well, I'm glad you asked. You could say the invocation and closing benediction for the seminar."

"It would be an honor and pleasure! Please tell Professor Reaper that I will be ready Friday morning by 9:00 AM. Will this be okay?"

"That will be fine. The seminar begins on Saturday at 9 AM until 4 PM with lunch being served at noon. May I pass your number to Professor Reaper so that he can contact you when he is in route?"

Thank you, Heavenly Father. Prayer STILL works!!!

"YES!" Immediately I realized that I had spoken with way too much excitement.

"Well, okay, then. Good evening."

Look at God!!!! I did not even have to scheme up a reason to contact Mr. Man. God worked it out for my good.

<u>Chapter 13</u>
All Good Ain't of God

"Beloved, believe not every spirit, but try the spirits whether they are of God: because many false prophets are gone out into the world."
I John 4:1

*M*ama had a colossal fit when I announced that I would be going out of town for the weekend to Libertine. I told her about the seminar and invitation from Professor Shaw. She called my bluff and told me she knew it was that Reaper character I was going to see again. I tried to explain how Professor Shaw invited me and asked me to be in charge of the prayers for the event, but she was not buying it Mama even accused James of talking Professor Shaw into inviting me.

"Carrington Rebekah, please listen to me! I know Satan's work when I see it. This Reaper character is not good for you. There is more to him than meets the eye. His eyes hide a story.

"Mama, Professor Reaper is not the devil. Professor Shaw spoke highly of him and how good he has been for the students of Libertine. Please don't worry. I am going to be fine."

"My sweet child, all good ain't of God." With that she excused herself from the table.

"Papa, are you upset with me, too?'

"Caring, you are an adult. I can only love you no matter what and be here for you as long as our good Lord allows me to be." After cleaning the kitchen, I went to pack. I took extra time in making my selections and accessories. Mama was half right. I was going to do what Professor Shaw asked me to do, but I was also going to make the most of seeing James Reaper again. I fell asleep with the biggest smile on my face.

It seemed as if the week dragged, but Friday morning had finally arrived. I was up and dressed by 7 AM! I cooked Mama and Pop a big breakfast and prepared their coffee by the time they had awakened at their usual 7:30 time. Though Mama was appreciative, she was quiet as the hour of my departure crept closer. Finally, as if he had been waiting around the corner, there was a knock at the door at nine o'clock sharp. Pop answered the door and properly greeted James. Mama muttered a good morning and hugged me as if this would be the last time. Then, she quickly turned from me and went back to the kitchen.

"I love you, Mama!" I yelled as she disappeared out of sight.

"We love you, Caring. You all be careful. Get my baby back safely to me, Professor Reaper." Pop always made things better.

I enjoyed the ride back to my old stomping grounds at Libertine, but, perhaps, it was the company I enjoyed more. James, as he insisted I call him, told me about his dreams and divine vision to one day build a church that also served as a shelter, hospital, and even a mental facility. From the passion in which he spoke, I knew he had a heart for God and serving God's people.

He wanted to know everything about me, and literally said this to me. I told him about the mysterious circumstances of my birth, growing up without a father and one day, maybe, finding him; and how I often wondered if there are others who look like me. He seemed so intrigued that I had grown up without feeling the need to harass my mother about who my father truly was, what had happened between them that caused him to disappear ,and why my family never to spoke of him again.

"I guess it just baffles me, Carrington. Your mother being a woman of God and coming from such a faith rooted family, how could they not ever feel compelled to tell you who your father is and why he is no longer around? Don't you feel cheated?"

He had a look on his face that was new to me. It was a mix of disdain while trying to disguise it as concern, or perhaps I was reading too much into it.

"I think my family did what they felt was best for me. I do not know why, but I do know that my birth brought my mother happiness and, also, a lot of pain that she tried her best to shield me from for a very long time. She has never said it nor has she ever made me feel like I was the cause of her pain, but I've always known that I am a major part of it. I remind her of something or someone."

For a minute, I was staring off into my mother's pain-filled eyes. Even though she fights to hold on to her faith and joy, I can still see pain in her beautiful, sad eyes. I was jolted back to the present when we passed by the seminary and turned down this winding path. I knew the path was there but never knew what was at the end of it.

"Is this a new entrance to the school?" I nervously inquired.

James had been extremely quiet, himself, since my confession of being the product of my mother's pain. He seemed almost agitated as he made sharp turns and jerks of the wheel. I thought he was ignoring me because of his patience in answering my question.

Suddenly, as if he had come back from a far off place, he blinked and shook his head.

"No, Carrington. This is the way to my home. I love the seminary and the libraries, so I asked around about this lot of land behind it. The school made me an offer I couldn't refuse. Welcome."

Almost rehearsed, as he spoke the trail opened in to the most beautiful land I had laid my eyes on. There was a wrap-around drive way and a huge maple tree off to the side of it. The tree was even decorated with an old tire swing, the perfect place for a child's tree house.

I was not sure where that thought had come from, but this place made me dream of things I did not even think I wanted. James, ever the gentleman, opened the passenger door and escorted me out of the car. I could tell he was pleased with my reaction to his home. I tried to look nonchalant but could not disguise the wonder and excitement.

"Go ahead; look around. I know you will find the backyard just as beautiful. Come in the house when you get ready. I'll unload your things."

"Wait! Unload my things? I am supposed to stay with Professor Shaw, James." I was confused, and my heart was racing a mile a minute. I can NOT stay with this man. I can NOT stay with this man. My mother would drive all the way here to kill me if she found out I was staying with this man.

James continued to unload my belongings as he spoke.

"Carrington, Professor Shaw has a family, so I thought it would be more comfortable for everyone if you stayed in my guest room. It's okay. No one is going to tell your mother." He winked when he mentioned my mother, which I did not find amusing at all.

"I am a grown woman, thank you, Professor Reaper. I just wish someone had informed me about the changes to my accommodations." With that, I headed toward the back of the house. When I reached the corner of the beautiful modest brick and stone residence, James called my name with a sexiness I knew was intentional.

"Carrington, I can see that you are indeed a FULL...grown...woman." Just like that he left me blushing as he disappeared behind the trunk of the car.

He had been modest when he spoke of the backyard. It looked like it had been torn out of a tourism magazine. Extending from the backyard was a deck that was decorated like the patios in Southern Living magazine. The private lake was bordered on the right and left by trees that looked as thouh they were covered in gold because of this time of year. It's flow was halted by the side of a huge boulder, affectionately known as 'The Rock' by students of the seminary. It was a place of peace and tranquility. I could have stared at this awesome masterpiece forever, but I heard it again. The gentle, sultry call of my name. Not wanting to seem too anxious, I counted to ten before retreating to his voice.

Walking back toward the house, I could see that the patio was just as thoughtfully decorated as the deck. James took my hand and moved to the side as I finally stepped into his home. Immediately I saw family time in front of the fireplace. What is wrong with you, Carrington? Get it together girl. You barely know this man.

"Welcome home, Carrington."

Always telling on myself with my facial expressions, I tried to turn away before he witnessed my startled countenance. Either, I moved too slowly or he was just quicker than me.

"I apologize. Welcome to my home, Carrington," he recovered calmly.

Still holding my hand, James led me on a silent tour of his home. In every room, I found myself easily imagining the things that would take place if I were the lady of the house. Entering his bedroom, I had to quietly repent for the things that had come to mind. I knew the Lord was not pleased in that moment, and the flesh was attempting to act up right along with my mind. I turned away and ran right into this stallion's chest. Not one to embarrass a lady, James turned and led me out of the room. Was it me, or did he take his time walking out of this room?

As we were headed upstairs, I saw a door at the end of the hall. Not wanting to disrupt this silent bonding we had going on, I tugged at James' hand. Gaining his attention, I nodded my headed toward the door.

"Carrington, that's just the basement. I'm embarrassed at how unorganized it is and wouldn't dare take you in it. It's just old discarded belongings from past and present. Nothing to see."

Flirting, I placed my hand on his chest.

"What types of things have you discarded from your past, Professor? Inquiring minds, want to know what"s underneath the layers."

"Oh, you will, in time, come to know all about me, my Dear. No worries about that, Beautiful."

He led me up the winding staircase to more bedrooms; four more to be exact. This house, I could easily see being the Reaper Family Home.

We would host our families and children's friends on different occasions throughout the year! Noooooooooo! Stop it, Carrington Rebekah. I had to shake these thoughts.

He led me to a room that was directly above the master bedroom downstairs, another Master Bedroom. This one was brighter, with a certain innocence in the tones that decorated it. The bed was almost as big as his downstairs, and the closet and bathroom were enormous. It would not take much to make this bedroom a studio apartment.

"These are your quarters, Carrington. I hope this will suit your taste." He looked around the room as if he was not sure that he had prepared it enough for my arrival.

"James, your home is exquisite. Your décor and style are impeccable! I would be comfortable sleeping on the bathroom floor!"

He laughed with a deep baritone, "Well,

glory to God, that won't be necessary."

After taking a long hot bath in my luxurious guest quarters, I dressed for dinner with the Shaws. All of sudden nothing I brought with me seemed befitting to wear while being escorted by a man of James Reaper's caliber. I did not want to look like the amateur that I was when it came to men of his status.

The guys I had even considered dating seemed like mere boys when compared to James.

What is wrong with me? Why was I thinking about this man like this?

As if on cue, there was a gentle knock on the door followed by his voice that I had come to daydream about.

"Carrington, I have something for you. May I come in?"

"Yes, you may, James." He had something for me.

I could not imagine what this "something" could be, which made me even more nervous.

Opening the door, he produced a moderately sized box with a blue ribbon tied on it. He held it out toward me with a nervousness I had never seen before.

I timidly accepted this surprise. I did not realize I had been holding my breath until   I opened the box and pulled back the tissue. Inside was a beautiful lace gown. Too shocked to go any further, James pulled the gown from the box as if were more fragile than usual.

"James, I...I don't know what to say," I stammered.

Holding it out before me, the floor length blue laced overlaid gown was gorgeous.

"Just say 'thank you," he responded.

"Thank you," I obediently responded. Laying the dress across the bed, he kissed my cheek and disappeared from the bedroom. Emerging from my room, I felt like a real woman. I felt a sexiness that I had never known I possessed. I felt powerful and confident. I had never known how much I had begun to look like my mother in her prime until I passed by the upstairs hall mirror to descend the stairs. My own reflection caught me so off guard that I instantly froze as if I had been caught sneaking out of the house by my mother.

It wasn't my mother. I slowly turned to face the mirror. My mocha skin, long black hair both came from my mother. Wow, my figure!!! Curves like her! Would my beauty be her curse or my blessing? Either way, I was now equipped with a new revelation: I was a grown woman, and I was ready to explore what that truly meant.

"Oh, my, Carrington, you are the picture of elegance. Blue is your color."

"Blue is my favorite color, James. I don't how you knew."

"Well, I know now. Shall we go?"

Dinner with Professor Shaw and his wife, along with a few other professors and their spouses, was amazing. Many of them remembered me as student and kindly presented me with unexpected praises. James looked onward with a look of pride and awe. I could not help but smile from ear to ear.

On the way back to his home, James and I chatted about the three invitations I had received to speak at a few of the professor's events. He seemed just as excited as I was about the exposure and opportunities the Lord seemed to be laying upon me. Finally, reaching the house, he cut the engine, and we continued laughing about the joke he had just told me. The laughter died down and the interior light faded out. I reached for the door with my right hand, and James grabbed my left.

"Carrington, please, wait. Let's walk to the dock. I need to tell you something, "he said pleadingly.

"James, it's getting late. We both have to be at the conference early tomorrow." I had to get space between us. My body temperature was rising, and I knew that every part of my body was aching to be close to this man. Any slight touch could spark a flame that would consume us both. No, no way, I could take the risk.

"Carrington, please. I just want to talk to you. Just talk." Looking into his beckoning face, I succumbed to his cry.

As we walked to the dock, he held my hand and carefully guided me along the path. The light from the light pole shined upon us with a soft warm glow. The moonlight reflected off of the water making the scenery the perfect place for a romantic scene.

Why was this happening? My mother knew he wanted more. Why didn't I just insist on my original plans to stay with the Shaws?

"James, what is it? Are you alright?" The sooner he told me what was going on the sooner I would be able to retreat to my private abode. Space is what I definitely needed to overcome this temptation to get close to this man.

"Carrington, I know we still have a lot to get to know about each other, but I can't help the way I feel. You are the answer to my prayer. You are the love that I have waited my entire existence for, and I want to hold on to that which I know God has allowed to place in my care."

"James." I was taken aback. Tonight had been full of surprises, but this? This was way more than I ever expected. What was he saying to me? It was almost as if he had read my mind because he answered that exact question.

"Carrington, what I am trying to say is that…..I've……fallen……..in love…….with you."

He made sure there was nothing to be confused or imagined. He made sure that I heard and understood every word.

"James." It was if time stood still. I was frozen in place. I couldn't think. This man. This beautifully created specimen. This highly respected man of theological and psychological circles had just said the words that had I never considered hearing at this time in my life. This man who was doing well for himself and could have any woman he wanted by his side had just confessed his love for me.

My stupor was one that could not be hidden by the darkness of the night. Taking my calling his name, I assume, as a cue for affirmation, James took my face in both of his hands and kissed me on my mouth. It was not aggressive, but the passion was there. Before I knew what was happening,   I was responding to his kiss with an equality of passion.

As soon as it had begun and before my body reacted, it was over. Slowly we walked and entered his home through the back door. Without any words spoken between us, James walked me to my bedroom door.

Kissing me once again, with the same passion but shorter duration, he hugged me close and went to his own room. Standing with my hand on the knob of my bedroom door, I confessed to myself with God as the only witness. I had fallen in love with James Reaper.

<u>Chapter 14</u>

Growing Pains

**"My son, forget not my law; but let thine heart
keep my commandments, for length of days,
and long life, and peace,
shall they add to thee."
Proverbs 3:1-2**

*F*rom the conference until my very last
day, James Reaper and I were inseparable.
It was obvious to others that our relationship had
taken a turn. Even Professor Shaw's wife and
another female professor, whom I had

grown quite close to in just a short while, had
noticed our magnetic attraction to one another.

"Carrington, I don't know how you did it, but
it is obvious that you did," Professor Shaw's wife,
Angela, stated.

"Angela, what are talking about? What have
I done?"

"Oh, come on, Carrington, that man's nose
is wide open! You have made THE James Reaper
fall in love! Girl, you have taken him off the market,"
Professor Sheila Tramwell exclaimed.

"Ladies, what are you saying? What do you
mean "THE" James Reaper? Are you saying he
has been the seminary Casanova, Sheila?"   I
decided not to disclose too much too fast. The
truth is, this weekend James and I had discussed
my moving back and getting married. We both
decided that this would be our decision and no
one else would get the opportunity to interfere.

Sheila explained, "Oh, no, nothing like that. It's just many women, myself included, have shown interest in this man only to be turned down flatly. He makes it very clear that he is not interested. He has never been rude which is probably what leaves the sting of his rejection." She laughed in good nature, but I could still tell she remembered the sting.

"Well, ladies, Professor Reaper and I are just allowing the Lord to direct our path. What will be, will be." I could not let on to what was truly happening between James and me. I felt like it was our own romantic fairytale. Anyone else would just taint our story; however, I couldn't help but wonder why he had chosen me.

The weekend went by in a blur. Knowing I had to return home weighed heavily on both of us. We barely spoke all the way back to Arkansas, but we held hands tightly the entire ride. Only when he had to make a turn did he let me go. Before I knew it, he was taking my bags from the car, as I headed to the steps of my mother's home.   It no longer felt like home. I was supposed to be with James.

Before I put my key in the lock, the door swung open, and I was in my mother's embrace.

"Thank You, Master, for bringing my baby back home to me. Thank You, Lord." I could hear relief in her voice but did not understand   it. She sounded as if I was just back from war.

"Hey, Mama, of course he brought me back.   I was only gone for a few days."

"Professor Reaper, How goes it, sir?" Pop had emerged from the house from somewhere. He greeted me with his normal hug and peck   on the forehead. Walking past me, he went to James and shook his hand. They walked up the stairs to the porch and went into the house together. Just when I went to follow, my mother placed her hand on the center of my abdomen.

"Carrington, something has changed. You have not lost your purity, but there is a change happening within you. Be careful, my girl." The intense look in her eyes explained the strength in her hand that was upon me. I don't know what this opposition was that was rising in me that caused me to look directly in her eyes and say what I did. I saw the concern, but I could not resist.

"I am a woman. I am my mother's daughter." With nothing left to say about the subject, I moved past her hand and entered the house.

"Hello, Lady Larain. I brought your daughter back safely and soundly." James was sincerely attempting to start a conversation with my mother, but she was not having it.

"You did bring her back, Professor Reaper. The condition in which you returned her has yet to be seen." She was cold and calculating. She was my mother and still the hint of distrust that she had always had about men, except for Pop, was there.

"Well, see we shall," James returned. Caught completely off guard by his counter to my mother's response, I had to remember how to shut my mouth. Much to my surprise, he sounded just as cold and calculating as she did. While it caused me some slight discomfort, I couldn't help but be a little thrilled that there was someone who had stood up to my mother's intimidation. I had not seen someone stand toe to toe with her and leave the room the same way they had come. My man. Professor James Reaper was in no way a push over.

"You have quite a drive, Professor Reaper. Safer to drive during the day when you can see what's coming your way. Thank you, again." It was easily understood to all that this was his warning to leave.

"The dark doesn't scare me. The Lord is my light and my salvation; whom shall I fear? the Lord is the strength of my life; of whom shall I be afraid?" Again, his tone was not disrespectful but direct and firm. "Pastor invited me to stay for dinner. I have heard you are the best cook in these parts. I would like to decide for myself, if that's alright with you, ma'am."

Right on time, Pop came from down the hall. "Alright, Til, I think it's time to eat, or it's time for me to eat!" He let out a hearty laugh and herded us to the table.

Dinner would have been in total silence had it not been for James and Pop who totally ignored Mama's stone face and silent disposition. I sat there feeling suffocated by the tension between the two of us that included dagger stares in James' direction. James and Pop discussed everything from church to politics. They seemed to enjoy themselves without worry or care about Mama's obvious dislike of James and outright hate at the thought of there being anything between him and me.

"Lady Larain, you are truly the best cook. It has been a honor to sit at your table. I must start on my journey now." My mama said not a word.

She stood from the table and walked into the kitchen. Pop and I walked James to his car. I was only silent to reserve the strength to hold my tears back.

What was going to happen? Would he still feel the same? Would he still want the same things we spoke when he returned without me?

"Pastor Luji, I must confess and ask you something extremely important." Suddenly, James seemed serious and focused. My heart begin to pound. Surely, he was not...........

"I am very much in love with Carrington. I know she is the woman I want to spend my life with, and I want your blessing. "I could not believe this was happening. Did he not know the potential danger he was in with Mama close by. I knew even though she was not in plain sight, she was listening to every word. I didn't realize that I was holding my breath until Pop spoke.

"Son, that's mighty humble of you, but I won't just give you a blessing such as this without speaking with my wife. I am not saying no because you are an adult, just as Carrington, and you will do what you want to do, but if you want my blessing you will just have to wait."

"I understand, sir. I appreciate your honesty, and yes, sir, you are right. We are adults. Though your blessing means a great deal to me, Carrington and I are two God-fearing adults. Ya'll have a great evening."

I knew James Reaper would be my husband; I just did not know when. One thing I did know was that I was not looking forward to a conversation with my mother.

Tamara S. La Guins

<u>Chapter 15</u>
The Beginning of the End

"And He said, "See to it that you are not misled; for many will come in My name, saying, 'I am He,' and, 'The time is near ' Do not go after them."
Luke 21:8

*T*o my surprise, my mother and Pop did not ask to have a conversation. My mother came to me one night with her stand-still position on the matter after she and Pop had spoke about James' confident explanation about where he was headed with me.

"Carrington, I am going to say what I think and feel, and I want you to hear me and hear me good. I know that you are an adult, but Baby, I was called to be your mother for a reason. You are in danger. You were conceived in rage and shame, justified by revenge, and carried and birthed by pain- A product of my pain- but you are also anointed by the power of God. A power that causes men to tremble and others to envy. There is a price to be paid because of what your father did and what was done about what your father did, and the devil is seeking it through you. Be careful, my girl, James Reaper is not all he appears to be. NO, I do not have proof, but I have a God who has never lied to me. He has warned me that James Reaper is a harm more so than a hindrance and is up to no good. IF you don't want to heed the warning of the very God you say called you from your own mother, then, daughter you do what you will, but you will REAP what you sow; as we all will. James Reaper was sent to make sure of that."

With those last heart-wrenching words, she turned and left me in my room to ponder what this prophetess had delivered to me. In my heart, I knew my mother loved me and had a truly extraordinary relationship with God, but I loved that man. I was in love with James Reaper and only saw love in his eyes. I had to go. It was time to grow up. The next time she heard from me, I would be Mrs. Carrington Rebekah Reaper. All that I needed to tell her, there was no way I was emotionally capable of saying to her face, I wrote it in a letter. I taped it to my bedroom door when I heard my parents retire for the night. Then, I left the home that I had called home for the majority of my days. I hated to leave this way, but I knew my mother and I had gone as far as we could with the issue. There were secrets she would never tell to help me understand who she was in all sincerity, and I was becoming a woman she could no longer protect no matter how hard she tried to keep me bound in the locked part of her heart. I had to live. This was my beginning; I just didn't consider what it might begin.

Quietly opening my parents' bedroom door, I soaked in the sounds of Pop's snoring and Mama's heavy breathing. I inhaled the smell of Mama's lavender fragrance and Pop's Old Spice aftershave. The love that I felt for James was so intense that is surprised me. I didn't know I had that much more to give, but I did and was ready to give it to James. I blew a silent kiss and gently closed the door.

Tiptoeing to the front door, I wondered if this was the feeling the teens had when they secretly spoke about the rush of sneaking out of the house. As I turned the knob, and slowly opened the door, I dared not look back over my shoulder for fear of my courage beening pulled from me. Taking a deep breath, I crossed over the threshold of home to the outside where the world and my future husband were waiting for me. Just as I was about to close the door on my childhood and all of it's memories, I thought I heard my mother's voice, "Abba, protect my daughter."

Throwing the door open, "Mama?" I saw no one in the darkness of the living room.

Closing the door, I stepped off the porch and walked into James' arms. He held me as though he felt the totality of strength this was taking. He placed me in the car as if I was his most fragile possession and proceeded to place all of my belongings in the trunk of the car. Then, he just stood there looking toward the front door.

Only God was witness to this standoff between good and evil. Only God knew who belonged to which side. Only God saw my mother on the other side of that window, standing with darkness all around her, staring my husband down with a look of distrust, disdain, and knowing what he was bringing into existence. While she stared at who she believed was a demon's spawn, and saw the smug, cryptic smile that creeped across his face, I stared straight ahead in darkness and wondered about what the light ahead possessed for my future. I would soon find out, but what price would have to be paid?

James entered the car and squeezed my hand.

"Carrington, there's no turning back." He didn't even wait for a response. Letting go of my hand, he drove us into the night.

Continue to Read the Series ...

Product of My Mother's Pain 2
Reaping What You Sow

About Author

Dr. Tamara S. La Guins had a tumultuous start in life, but through ex those traumatic experiences, God became a her close friend.   She credits her journey with fueling her dreams of becoming best-selling author and actress and answering to the call of evangelism and service to God's people. Believing knowledge is power, she has degrees in Counseling and Divinity.   Dr. La Guins is a mentor and spiritual leader for those who are broken, afraid, and angry because of their past or present situations and circumstances, and is continues to work in the field of Education.

She lives in Georgia with her husband, children, and dog; all she describes as her grace-given blessings.   If she is remembered for nothing else, she wants to be remembered as a Child of God.

Pure Thoughts Publishing, LLC

www.ingramcontent.com/pod-product-compliance
Lightning Source LLC
Chambersburg PA
CBHW050748250626
47155CB00005B/1979

* 9 7 8 1 9 4 3 4 0 9 7 3 0 *